Bedtime Poems

to read to your new baby

in the womb or in your arms

J. M. Vantes

Bedtime Stories
By J.M. Vantes
Copyright 2014

Published by Two Princes Books and Publishing

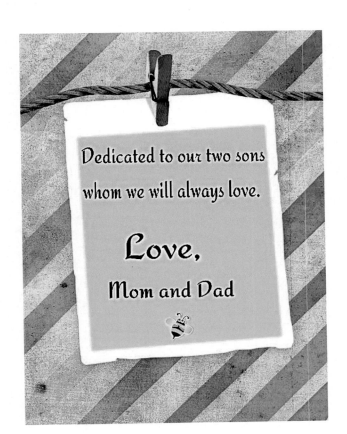

Dedicated to our two sons whom we will always love.

Love,

Mom and Dad

At first I couldnt believe it, But then I knew it to be true.

Deep inside my belly was you.

Then I was sleeping in my bed,
From within I felt a special knock.
I wish I could hold your little head,
Asleep in my lap gently while I rock.

As the day finally
draws near
For me to see your
face,
I will push until
your cry I hear
Then hold you
close with grace.

Little Baby inside my womb
I can hear your heart beat fast
Like a racecar goes "vroom!"
Little Baby I'll love you
even if you finish last.

Little Baby how are you now?
Calmly you wander and roam
Grazing for a little food
like a cute baby cow.
I hope you like it inside your
little home,
Little Baby I'll love you forever
I Solemnly vow.

My sweet little baby
Do it again I know you can
Are you playing soccer maybe?
Can I be your biggest fan?

I feel those big kicks
I feel every shot you make
Pros, see what's new in the mix
This little one will shake the field
Like an earthquake!

Little Baby play all day long
When you are ready for bed,
I'll sing you a song.

Awaiting You

Dearest little one I love
You are my truest of breaths
My heart awaits for your
hugs I won't get enough

I'll hold you as long as you
let me with these arms
of depth

Awaiting your days to come
I lie here and wonder
Do you hear the poems we tell you
or the songs we hum?
Do we sound like two people or
the rain and thunder?
I hope you know the love we
have and its sum

I love you

When You Grow Up

One of these days you'll grow up tall
Some day you may be bigger than Mom
The world can be tough but don't worry,
If you fall
Hang in there it takes time,
just keep calm
I can see it now, you'll show them all.

When you're older and grow up big
You'll go out and get your first job
You can be a banker or rock star with a gig
In the crowd you'll see me in the mob

I don't care what you do
As long as you work hard
The future is up to you
Maybe you'll join the Coast Guard,
but never give up; I'll see you through.
Life may make you cry or smile

Every day will be something new
Believe me it's worth your while
You will always have me to talk to
So don't worry, you can handle any mile.

You have the greatest smile I have ever seen
It lights up the days better than the sun ever could
Your smile is warm, happy, perfect, and serene
It makes the night sky shine where the stars never would
My child your smile blossoms like tulips in Spring
It is the best part of my days; your smile inspires
everything good

As a baby your smiles were so cheerful, you would gleam
As you grew a little older your smiles showed
meaning and livelihood

And as you keep growing those smiles show me
you are happy and we did all right,
it seems

Hard to imagine a love could ever die
It seemed eternal and complete
Next to no one else would you lie
But like a cat you'll land on your feet
Again a twinkle will show in your eye

One day the sun will set
All will go dark and grey
Everything will hurt but don't fret
Everything will then get better I say

Someone special will hold your heart
They'll make you happy and alive
Together you're a perfect piece of art
Without each other you cannot thrive

One day the sun will shine
So bright you won't see straight
Nothing will be so divine
Nothing will feel so great

It's new and exciting, a special time
You've never experienced this before
You blend like sweet lemon and lime
Inseparable in one embrace, forever more

The grass has never been greener
Every song is sung so lovely
The whole world in romantic demeanor
Every kiss planted so gently

A simple hug leaves you breathless
A glance will make you melt
Your bond is indestructible and endless
Passion and desire you've never felt
Each day passes, each minute priceless

Even if it ends, the memory withstands
Some are bad but cherish what's good
Think about the laughs and holding hands
When you meet another, try again you should
As you live and learn, your heart expands

When Your Heart First Breaks

There will be a wicked time in life
When another heart gives you pain
Your heart will ache with angst and strife
You will no longer feel as if you're dancing;
but left in the rain
When you first fall sad
Come to me and let me comfort you
We have all been hurt and plenty mad
Every heart breaks; just what we
all go through
But when the pain is over and through,
you'll notice all goes again to good from bad

Take the hurt you were given
And turn it into the strength you need
Right now it feels like betrayal,
revenge stricken
But don't stay that way, don't let
your sorrows breed
With those feelings of mistrust
let your emotions fade to be
rewritten

A time will come for a new face
A special addition will arrive
Your life will be set in a new pace
This little being needs you, to survive
Stand strong, carry extra diapers just in case!

As I did for you, you will now
I held and bathed you daily
Everything is tough at first but you'll learn how
To be a good parent to your baby
Congratulations to you, take a bow

Everyday will be something grand
New things to learn and experience
To try to sit up, crawl, walk, and stand
You'll see his or her innate perseverance
You will learn to love in a way you didn't know you can

A new chapter awaits from here
Good luck to you, life has changed forever
Enjoy the journey, have fun my dear
Embrace each moment of this new endeavor
Always say "I love you", whether far or near
And be unhappy, never ever

LOVE

I will love you before you are born

I will love you the day we first meet

I will love you ever more

I will love you when you can stand
on your feet

I will love you and adorn

When you can ride your bike in
the street

And as a teen with attitude and scorn

I will still love you my angel sweet

I will love you until you're old and

then some; you are my own

To Our Beautiful Bundle of Joy,

May you always know

you are wanted and loved.